The
OUTING

A Gay Christian's Journey Towards Self-Acceptance

JAMES D. DOLLINS

DEDICATION

To Paul Dodd who told me,
"Why don't *you* write it?"

— ACKNOWLEDGMENTS —

THANK YOU SERENA, my precious wife, for all of your encouragement and proofreading. Thanks to **Sue Laurie, Chad Heilig** and **Paul Dodd** who model courageous integrity as openly gay Christians. To **Eric Schulz** who helped me to move from prejudice to acceptance. To **Carl Morrison**, cover image photographer, **Mary and Don Decker**, editors, **David Wogahn** publishing consultant, and many others who graciously read this work and gave wise feedback.

CHAPTER 1

EVERYONE WAS WATCHING EVERYONE at that age. To wear a new pair of shoes to school was to wade into frigid waters. One had to wait long, cold moments to know if peers would appreciate or ridicule. Only then could he determine whether he would ever wear them to middle school again.

The boys Grant watched in search of role models. Some, but only a few, had an air of self-assurance that he envied deeply. Not until later in life would he see that these poised, witty elite had simply resolved, despite others' opinions, to accept themselves and to freely express their ideas.

The girls they all watched as exhibitions. Within six weeks or so they were assigned an appropriate rank among peers, judged first by beauty, then dress, then sense of humor and, finally, by intelligence. The girls were Grant's friends, and not a threat.

Nichole and Zoe had created an elaborate chewing gum mosaic on the concrete wall by their lockers close to Grant's. Once, when Zoe blew a small bubble to pop in Grant's face, Grant grabbed it from her mouth and stuck it to the wall art before the bubble could deflate. Grant, being stronger, was able to defend against her playful effort to steal a pack of gum from his backpack.

When the wrestling was over, Grant looked one more time at their collective work of rebellious art on the cold wall. Despite himself, he could not resist glancing below the gum pieces where he saw the frightening words, "Rick is a fag."

Many times Grant had pondered whether the author of these words had been teasing a close friend, or threatening a future victim. He wondered whether the sentence was written the previous school year or long before that. Whatever the back story, the quickly scribbled words, penned with indelible blue ink, always left Grant with a sense of terror.

At this age, the fork in the road was becoming clear. Either you were gay or you weren't, and, for many, the truth bubbled inevitably to the surface during these years. Someone would notice the gait of a boy running down the basketball court and make a remark. They might even mimic him, jogging or skipping with an exaggerated bounce. Taunting words like those inked into that concrete wall were like bullets that would miss most people, but would hit a few. Everyone prayed that they would not hit them. Grant was not at all sure he could escape.

At the same time, Grant's male friends were envious of his friendships with girls like Zoe and Nichole. They wistfully confessed to Grant that they would do anything to be allowed into such close proximity with these beautiful, maturing girls. Disastrously, though, it was never the touch of these two, or of any other girl that commanded Grant's attention.

"Grant!" someone playfully called out, as a hand gripped his shoulder briefly but firmly from behind his back. Grant tensed to see Marco's bright smile speeding past him down the hallway. With the voice and touch, Grant felt his heart was lifted in his chest. He smiled, waved and turned back to his locker. Suddenly he could not remember which books and folders to choose for his next class. When he finally was ready to leave his locker, he glanced at the gum mosaic and avoided reading the words written below.

CHAPTER 2

TWO WEEKS LATER, on a Wednesday, Grant arrived at his church's front office to put in his time volunteering, as was required for his Confirmation Class. The church always seemed an old, stale place during weekdays, so different from the socially vibrant scene on Sunday mornings. It was a safe haven, though, a true sanctuary, and the office staff doted over Grant and his computer skills. Meredith, the receptionist, had begun leaving a can of Pepsi for him in the office refrigerator. Grant went straight to the kitchenette as he had done for several Wednesdays now.

Today Meredith asked Grant to install new publishing software on one of the office computers. This computer sat in a small, isolated office that seemed even quieter than the other rooms of the building. This was partly because it was adjacent to the senior minister's office, a space reserved for study and private conversations.

Grant knew, however, that the conversations were not private if a volunteer sat at this computer, especially when the old wooden sliding door joining the rooms was not completely closed. On entering the room, Grant could easily hear, through the door's quarter-inch opening, that a conversation was already in progress, and he didn't dare close it now. Soon, he caught several intriguing exchanges between his pastor, Mike Norquist, and another man, who spoke with Pastor Norquist like a peer.

As Grant downloaded software from a compact disk, a slow process on this out-dated computer, he distinguished the hushed tones of two ministers discussing something that sounded serious. It was as though they were hashing out some disagreement, but carefully preserving congeniality in their tone. Pastor Norquist's visitor seemed to implore Pastor Norquist to see things his way. For quite a while Grant heard nothing voiced by his own pastor in response.

Pastor Norquist tended to listen and to think a lot before weighing in on important issues.

Eventually, his visitor insisted, "Mike, I really want to know where you're at on this. To me the scripture is clear – however much we should love our gay friends and neighbors, God cannot condone a homosexual lifestyle."

The software was nearly finished downloading, but these last words fixed Grant to his seat. He would not get up before hearing his pastor's response.

It came after a few seconds' pause. "Dave, what I always come back to is Jesus. I just can't imagine that he would care very much about whom people choose to love. And we are talking about love, after all. So often we speak of gay relationships as though they are only about sex. I'd never want people to think of my own marriage in that way. So much of a couple's love has nothing to do with sexual relations. It's love! And the Bible always seems to honor true love. I just think we had better be careful not to call something sinful or deviant when we may find that it's really a sacred, God-given grace."

The pauses between the two men's comments grew longer after that. The conversation was no longer about ethics only, but perhaps about a friendship as well.

"I can't say that I'm surprised," said the guest. In the 20 years I've known you, you've always come down on the side of compassion toward others."

"That's generous of you, Dave," Pastor Norquist responded slowly. "And you have always stood up for the integrity of God's law. I respect that too; I hope you understand."

"I do, Mike. Listen, may I offer a prayer?"

With this, Grant's sense of guilt for eavesdropping finally outstripped his curiosity, and he got up to leave the small office. But first, he decided to finish installing the program. This required restarting the computer, which was a foolish idea, because the "shutting-down" tune would soon sound. As Grant stepped out the door, he was mortified to hear how loudly the melody was played, and he cursed whatever volunteer it was who had left the volume so high.

Grant walked directly to the counter where he had placed his soda and tried to look occupied while Pastor Norquist walked down the hallway with his friend and then out the door toward the parking lot. Soon, the pastor came back in and said, as Grant straightened a stack of flyers, "So, sounds like you're working on our computers again today!" Grant looked up and saw a familiar hint of humor in the man's expression, an honesty that did not seem at all threatening. Grant felt his confidence return. He also noticed a look of fatigue in the pastor's face, like that of someone who had taken a trip and found it to be much longer than he expected.

"Yes, the publishing program should be ready to use now. I probably need to turn down the volume on those speakers, though."

"They are a little loud," answered the pastor, now fully smiling as he stepped down the hallway toward the kitchenette.

Grant knew he didn't need to confess, but he felt compelled to follow the pastor anyway. He walked into the small kitchen area as Pastor Norquist was pouring a cup of coffee.

"Can I ask you something?" Grant said.

Pastor Norquist's eyes widened, but continued to focus on the coffee he was now stirring. "Of course, Grant." Behind the pastor's welcoming words, Grant again detected that he felt winded. "But let's go sit down, O.K.?"

Grant had never done this before. He followed his parents' lead at church, dressed handsomely on Sunday mornings, and spoke insightfully in Sunday School. He was able, with wit and charm, to be perceived as a well-adjusted and respectable youth of the church.

Yet today he felt emboldened to ask other questions on his own terms – the kind of discussion that would have dissolved his self-assurance if it were held in front of his peers. Suddenly this new conversation felt oddly like a time of confession. He realized that the subject at hand was more than the hit-and-run, one-question, one-answer conversation he had hoped it could be.

Once they were seated, Grant ventured, "If the Bible says homosexuality is wrong, then Christians can't accept homosexual people, right? Or at least they're not supposed to." Grant was surprised at the tone of his own voice which suddenly took on a harsh, almost accusatory sound.

Pastor Norquist seemed to hear the accusation before he could hear the question. He sensed Grant's agitation and discomfort with this conversation which Grant seemed so compelled to begin. He knew Grant well enough to trust the intentions of his heart. He also saw that his visitor was afraid, so that he might either attack or flee if things went badly. Pastor Norquist dearly wanted, above all, to avoid a meltdown.

He tried hard to convey a calming presence. "You bring up a very important question, Grant. And I know I stand on difficult footing when I claim that Christians must be more tolerant of gays. There are a number of verses in the Bible that people can point to that condemn homosexual behavior. A gay Christian friend of mine once called these the 'clobber verses' because they're often quoted to gays and lesbians to prove that they're sinful. If you'd like, I can explain my belief about those scriptures."

Grant didn't feel like sitting through a Sunday School lesson. His heart was pumping hard. He guessed that Pastor Norquist must assume by now that he was gay, and this was something Grant was not willing to assume for himself. But, out of respect, he tried to remain attentive. "Sure, I'd like to hear it."

"OK." Pastor Norquist paused to think before he spoke. He was aware that his answer might sound shallow, merely theoretical, if spoken in a room with someone who wrestled personally with the question.

He began, "The words, 'homosexuality' and 'sexual orientation' are never mentioned in the Bible. It seems, when we carefully read scripture, that homosexual behavior was assumed to be abnormal, but scripture never speaks of homosexuality as something inherent in people. The same goes for heterosexuality, for that matter. Perhaps in the New Testament, when St. Paul counsels people to marry if they can't be chaste, he's acknowledging that some people are not meant to be celibate. But that's about as close as the Bible gets to describing sexual orientation as something inherent in each person's being."

Grant was trying to hold on to the pastor's logic. He didn't entirely follow him. Still, it was clear that this mattered enough to Pastor Norquist that he felt obliged to give a thorough explanation.

"I don't want to bore you, Grant, but through the friendships I've had with gay people, and in more and more of the material I read, it truly seems that some people in the world are simply born gay. At some point, I accepted that if God has made people either straight or gay, it's not my job to judge that. In fact, I have felt increasingly called to accept gay persons for who they are, especially when they feel rejected by so many others. This is how Jesus treats marginalized people in the Bible, and I believe I'm called to do likewise."

His pastor's words were refreshing and unexpected. They were also puzzling. Grant sensed that there was not yet much room in his world for the perspective Pastor Norquist articulated. This concept was not something he could carry to school with him to be easily consumed by friends and strangers. He realized now that, when he'd entered the pastor's office, he had entertained only two options – acceptance or rejection of homosexuals. He didn't expect his pastor to both discuss the Bible with respect, and then to second-guess certain biblical passages.

At this point, Grant felt he could no longer form a complete sentence without allowing himself more time to thoroughly process his pastor's words. He was also vaguely aware that he might be adding to the fatigue he had detected on Pastor Norquist's face earlier.

"Well, thank you, Pastor Norquist," he said. "This is a lot to chew on."

"I enjoy it," the minister responded warmly, standing up from his chair. "These are the conversations that I love the most." The words sounded genuine to Grant.

Saying his goodbyes to the ladies in the office, Grant smiled at how odd it was that such a staid, mundane building could feel strangely sacred.

CHAPTER 3

GRANT'S BIKE RIDE HOME helped to settle the intense questions stirred up in his talk with Pastor Norquist. His mother greeted him at the door to tell him that he was invited to spend a week in the mountains that summer at the home of his uncle. Next to his parents, and perhaps now his minister, Uncle Chapman, or "Chap," was one of the adults Grant trusted most.

Chap was a recluse, but one with a wide range of interests and talents – fishing, painting, gourmet cooking and poetry. Chap's sister, Grant's mother, spoke of her brother as someone who was too sensitive to live in a city. When Grant asked her what she meant by this, she thoughtfully answered, "He seems to be overwhelmed by too many humans in too small a space." Apparently, Chap much preferred the occasional encounter with rural neighbors whom he could adequately appreciate, one by one. So he accepted the rumors that he was a misfit in exchange for the opportunity to express himself on his own terms to fewer acquaintances.

It was an honor, then, for Grant to be admitted into Chap's circle of human interaction. More than an honor, it was a relief for Grant to daydream of a second home where he could let his own scattered thoughts settle.

Summer finally arrived, and Grant gratefully traveled in the passenger seat of his mother's car, reviewing the beautiful scenes he'd watched mostly during weekend family visits to see Uncle Chap. Grant's mother did not speak much as she drove. Normally she was extroverted and the initiator of conversations with others. But over the past year or two she'd observed Grant becoming more reflective and, increasingly, felt inclined not to disturb the space that his pensiveness created, however lonely it made her feel.

So, as the car turned in to the smaller dirt road leading to Chap's cabin, the script for mother and son was starkly quieter than the bouncy banter she remembered sharing with her son at this point in the trip when he was a boy.

As was his habit, Chap was seated on his front porch reading when they reached the cabin. His eyes lit up as he rose and smiled at the car. Chap's greeting seemed to Grant a warm but gradual gesture. He welcomed his visitors as a movie-goer welcomes daylight upon exiting the theater. Though he loved these two guests as deeply as any others, it was all Chap could manage to allow the population of his homestead to triple.

Sensitive to this, Grant's mother established that she would leave after dinner, and she did. The meal itself did not require much time, a simple and delicious repast of greens from Chap's garden accompanied by a rich stew with herbs that had been scenting the cedar cabin's kitchen all day long. Chap then served some tea and cake and, soon after, with a couple of hugs and not many more words, the house was left with only two.

Chap prepared a second plate of cake for both of them and poured two more cups of tea. He brought these into the warmly lit living room where Grant was already sitting in his customary place on the couch. They sat, ate and drank until someone felt like speaking.

"So, Chap," Grant began, "Why didn't you ever get married?" Grant's family had always been impatient with small talk. Between that tradition and Grant's anxiousness to learn more about human relationships, the question seemed more than appropriate. Besides, Grant figured that Chap, a good-looking and endearing man, would have had the option to wed at some point and wouldn't feel embarrassed to answer.

"I did." He paused to observe Grant's reaction. "I guess your mom never told you."

"No, I had no idea."

Chap took another sip of tea and settled deeper into his chair. He was accustomed to such mature talk from his thirteen-year-old nephew. Grant's family spent the night at Chap's home about two or three times a year on holiday weekends and for day hikes during summers. When Grant's family spent the night,

Chap would always insist that the parents sleep in his own double bed. Chap would take advantage of the arrangement to set up his beloved canvas cot on the back porch under the stars. Grant and his younger sister slept on twin beds in Chap's small guest room, or, weather-permitting, outside with Chap.

Either at mealtime or during "pillow talk" under the stars, the kids were allowed and encouraged to float big thoughts in conversation with their elders. There was a delightful, tacit understanding among the adults that they should not flinch or gawk at precocious ideas or sophisticated vocabulary contributed by Grant or his sister. In this arrangement, it was also expected that the adults might take their time responding to the children's questions as Chap was doing now.

"It was too much for me, Grant. I suppose it's too much for many people, judging by the success rate. But I didn't handle fights well. There are lots of things I could have done better. Sometimes I think we didn't try hard enough to make it work, I don't know. I do thank God we never brought any children into the picture. In less than two years it was all over."

Grant scanned the cabin for signs of a past marriage. He didn't see any.

"You could have remarried, though, Chap," Grant ventured. "I don't want to pry, but couldn't you have learned from those mistakes and tried again?"

"I guess it's just not my thing, Grant. People bring such intensity to romance. They often expect nothing less than salvation out of the deal. I imagine I'd be swept up in that again, tumbled around and washed half-dead onto shore like I was the first time." Chap set down his teacup and focused his eyes forward, digging deeper for some wisdom that might honor Grant's brave questions.

"The couples I respect are the ones who have outlasted all those storms and are still standing – together. There's true beauty in that, in the warm, accepting soul who's sharing your living space, sharing with you the daily rituals: coffee, newspaper, walking. This culture has people fooled into believing that love's all about passion and romance. I suppose it's not as exciting, but true love's about companionship. Sometimes I do find myself pining for a companion." Chap's words conveyed thoughts that had passed through his mind many times before. The sound of them suited the appearance of his weathered face.

"And what about you, Grant?" Chap smirked. "Have you set your sites on some girl at school, or church?"

"Grant forced a smile, "No, Chap, I guess that's not really my thing either."

Chap noted Grant's decisiveness and brevity in answering, and quietly focused on his cup of tea. Again this topic led to more intensity than Chap was ready for. His own wistful musings contrasted starkly with the apparent urgency of Grant's quiet quandary. Now he would content himself with a moment of gracious, honest silence.

At the right moment, Chap continued, "Would you like to go on a hike tomorrow? The AmeriCorps kids cleared a new trail up to one of the peaks."

"Yeah, of course, Chap."

"I'll get you up at seven. You might want to hit the hay soon. Good night, bud."

"Night Chap."

Chap crossed the room, and with a kiss to Grant's forehead, he retired to his own room to sleep.

CHAPTER 4

JUST AS GENTLY, Chap roused Grant early the next morning to the rich smells of bacon and coffee. Grant awoke slowly, as though hung-over from the weighty conversation nine hours before.

The two fed themselves, laced their hiking boots and, while the mist of the morning was still thick, set out for the trail. They each carried minimal weight – a canteen and a daypack containing a small snack.

The trail head was located just one half mile from Chap's home, at the border of a state wilderness preserve. With his uncle leading, Grant would usually rest from thinking about directions, but today he felt less like a child than on previous visits. He paid attention to landmarks along the way.

Chap and Grant were not chatty hikers. Chap was more prone to interact with the exceptional bugs and wildflowers than to exploit the opportunity for quality conversation. This left space for Grant's mind to review the ideas exchanged last night.

He had never considered different qualities of love before. He understood now that Chap had chosen to forgo a certain version of love. Chap had given up on the expectation that love must be thrilling and intense, as Grant had heard it described in the lyrics of love songs. Some of those ballads portrayed being in love as the pinnacle of all human experience. Some songs went even further, describing that bond as some sort of blood-pact between two people who, without each other, would surely die.

Grant reflected on Chap's alternative model, romantic companionship, and wondered how such love might fit his own life. Grant's friendships with Nichole and Zoe supported and strengthened him, but such friendships would never become any kind of permanent commitment.

He recalled the touch of Marco on his back in the school hallway. That was a feeling that could hold his interest much longer. He did not know Marco well, but he also could not rule him out as an imagined life-long, romantic friend.

This day-dreamed love strangely fit Grant's imagination of the future. Nothing else did, though. Chap's notion of unselfish, romantic companionship suited Chap perfectly, but it would never replace the adventure of teenage love. Grant could not practice such disciplined love in middle school any more than he could wear one of Chap's musty flannel shirts to class.

Likewise, however gracious a man Pastor Norquist may be, if Grant ever brought a romantic friend such as Marco to church, there would be few people besides the pastor who would be ready with the same openness of mind and heart.

Just like his uncle, Grant would set aside his hopes for love, at least until the odds seemed better that he could realize them.

The hiking refreshed him. Though he would put segments of his life indefinitely on hold, no one could keep Grant and his uncle from walking to whatever peak they chose. As always, Chap selected the right trail for the season so that blooms and creatures revealed themselves as if placed there on display. When they reached the peak, Chap indicated the continuation of the trail down the mountain's opposite side.

"That's the dry side of the mountain, much more of a desert, really-- whole different vegetation and wildlife. That's why I live on this side," Chap quipped. The trail goes down to Larkspur. They've got a church, a bar and a really good malt shop, and that's about it. In a couple of years you and I can hike the whole thing. We'd need to carry some more food to do it though."

Grant guessed that he could hike it now but didn't answer Chap's underestimation of his strength. He did not want to contradict anyone now. He just wanted to be. The entire day he had observed creatures and foliage that could live just as they were made. They were true to their instincts and survived by them.

Those living things left him alone. Grant imagined that he was accepted here-- that birds, lizards and insects were not smart enough, or foolish enough, to judge him or any other creature.

"Ready to go back down?" Chap asked.

"I guess so."

When they returned to Chap's house, Grant confirmed to himself that he could have walked much farther. Soon he felt restless in a way that made it difficult to concentrate on the leisurely, intelligent evening of conversation that Chap had to offer.

After their simple, delicious dinner and a hot chocolate, Grant said he might retire early or do some reading. But his mind dismissed resting or reading as readily as it had rejected a talk with Chap. He suddenly thought only of the day to come and fell in love with a new idea. He forced himself to go to bed early, impatient for the morning to arrive.

Right around four in the morning, Grant's brain awoke him as he had told it to. He knew that Chap was a light sleeper, but that he was also a creature of habit and would normally not wake up until six. Grant treaded lightly through his room in socked feet and loaded his school backpack with basics only: his pocketknife, a spare sweatshirt, matches that he found on the dresser, and then he headed to the kitchen.

Grant hoped Chap would not resent that some food and one of his favorite canteens would be missing. Chap owned the perfect stuff for an adventure. Grant stocked his pack with granola, locally-made jerky and fruit. He was pleased, too, to fill the canteen with the kitchen tap water. This water was pumped from a well and tasted much purer than the city water Grant had been raised on.

Next, Grant took paper and pen and wrote, "Chap, I went for a hike. I'll be back for dinner. Please don't worry. Love, Grant." He taped the note above the kitchen faucet. Gingerly closing the kitchen door behind him, Grant traversed Chap's dirt driveway and set out for the trail.

Without pauses to notice the trail's flora and fauna, Grant made excellent time. The chill and humidity of the air quickly took over his senses and caused him to forget the initial guilt he had felt over betraying the trust of both Chap and, ultimately, his own parents.

His enchantment with the morning was heightened by a sense of courage that felt new. This trip would have been a reckless one had he taken it two years ago, or even last year. Now it was certainly rebellious, but not haphazard. He felt prepared, beyond his provisions, for this expedition.

Three months earlier, Grant was told he could now claim his religious belief for himself. At church, he and his Confirmation classmates were taught that they were no longer children whose piety would be managed by their parents. Grant and his friends had stood before the congregation and professed their own faith. Grant meant those words as he said them, and he remembered that day with gratitude and warmth.

He was now trusted to form his own beliefs and, consequently, his behavior. So it would be ironic if his parents would condemn the decision he had boldly made this morning. He was entering a time when he knew he had the knack of living his own life and of making decisions for himself. It wasn't that he knew it all, but he did know enough. Even better, his physical ability harmonized with the confidence of his mind and emotions. He passed this milestone of autonomy in one fleeting moment. He did not reflect on it further, but felt driven to reach the peak.

As he expected, Grant summited the mountain early. Alone, he was able to make fast progress while still taking in the scents of sage brush and the dew drying on the grasses. Grant's mind, his lungs, the dirt trail and each living thing around him seemed to affirm that he was in the right place. He felt invited to be here.

The same sensation urged him to descend the other side of the mountain toward Larkspur.

But first, Grant mentally retraced his steps and guessed that Chap was probably a good enough tracker to find him here. He had left the note for Chap to prevent him from panicking, but he also wanted badly to have enough time to travel as far as he needed to. If Chap decided that his nephew was too young for this adventure, he might cancel Grant's journey before it could be completed.

So, he stepped off the trail, leaving clear footprints, until he came to an expansive granite surface on the mountainside. He traversed the fractured rock for over 100 feet and then jumped down onto piles of leaves under the branches of a giant oak. The leaves were thick enough for Grant to kick them back over the places where he stepped. He continued walking and rearranging leaves until he reached the opposite side of the branches' perimeter. Looking back, he felt confident that his prints would be screened from anyone who might look out from the granite rock. He continued in a straight line back toward the place where he assumed the trail would continue.

He was thrilled to see he had guessed correctly. The AmeriCorps trailblazers had created the path using switchbacks, so Grant was easily able to find the trail again halfway down the steep hillside. He noted that, as he resumed walking on a trail, his hiking boots did leave clearly identifiable prints. But there was surely enough distance from his point of departure from the trail to slow Chap down considerably, though probably not enough to shake him entirely from the search.

Now he turned his thoughts to the malt. Chap should have known better than to mention a malt shop to his teenage nephew, Grant thought. The reward that awaited him seemed to be yet another sign that Grant's journey was meant to be. He descended toward Larkspur, stopping occasionally to eat jerky and granola from his daypack. As he continued easily downhill, he welcomed every stretch of the dry, eastern mountainside.

Eventually, the trail merged with a concrete sidewalk as he entered Larkspur. Grant felt more conspicuous than he'd ever felt before. He noticed that a man who was sitting in a gas station across the street was watching his every step. Grant felt self-conscious about the way he walked anyway-- he always had, but more so now, so that each step had to be reinvented as he took it.

A single green car sat poised to enter the main strip from a convenience store parking lot. As it idled, the engine rumbled powerfully, but low. For a moment, Grant allowed himself to admire the metallic green finish, framed by meticulously polished chrome. Then he glanced at the passengers inside. Two older teenagers gazed at Grant from opposite ends of the car's long front bench seat. The moment after Grant made eye contact with the driver, the rear wheels chirped and squealed, and the engine thundered, propelling the car out onto the main street. It was all Grant could do to keep walking.

Thankfully, he soon sighted the neon word "Malts" in a large glass window. It was 1:30 now, and Grant was ready to celebrate this humble destination.

CHAPTER 5

PERHAPS HE LOOKED LIKE A CHILD, or a mini-customer entering the Main Street Malt Shop. Grant felt himself shrink in stature, from a courageous explorer on the trail to an under-sized tourist of Larkspur. He began to feel desperate for a friendly face and was relieved to see a teenaged girl, slightly older than he, sitting on a stool behind the cash register, reading a book. She looked up and, smiling, said, "Have a seat."

Grateful to be treated as any other customer, Grant sat on one of the barstool seats and smiled back. It remained quiet while the girl finished reading a paragraph, placed her bookmark and handed Grant a menu.

"Malt?" she asked.

Without consulting the menu, Grant asked for a chocolate one, and the girl set to work.

She seemed relaxed and Grant saw that she was very pretty, with brunette hair buzzed short in the back but left longer above her face.

The two fell easily into conversation. The malt was delicious. So was the independence. Her autonomy was entrusted to her by parents who let her run the shop Saturday mornings to earn spending money. Grant's freedom, of course, had been commandeered and would expire in a few more hours.

In the meantime, he shared ideas freely with Sophie, whose name also enchanted Grant when he learned it. And Sophie, enamored of Grant's wit and creativity, also shed her reserved appearance to laugh often and lean over the malt shop counter.

Grant and Sophie knew none of this could work if there were a scent of romance in the air. But both felt that there wasn't. Grant knew there would not be. And Sophie was aware, instinctually, that Grant would not begin to flirt with her.

A half hour into the conversation, Grant watched Sophie's face grow momentarily somber, and at the same moment, recognized the rumble of the green car's engine passing slowly behind him.

"Do you know those guys?" asked Grant.

"It's my cousin and his friend. They're idiots. The car seems to make them act even more stupid. Don't pay them any attention."

This sounded half like reassurance and half like strategic advice. Grant would make sure to follow it.

The two talked until 3:00 p.m., when Sophie was scheduled to get off work. Grant was especially embarrassed when he went to pay for his malt and found that it was much more expensive than he thought. He only had $4 in his wallet, and the malt cost $4.95. Again, he felt like a little child. Sophie didn't flinch. "Don't sweat it," she said, "I'll ring up a small one instead." She punched in $3.95 and gave him back a nickel "for the taxi home," she said.

"Yeah, I've got to start walking back to my uncle's house," he said.

"Let's go. I can close up now anyway. I'll show you where I live, OK?"

They remained in their blissful world of conversation as they walked down Main Street, and then the familiar rumbling of a car pulled them out of it. It approached them from behind and slowed, so that its idle tauntingly drowned out their words.

"Sophie, who's your gay boyfriend?" The passenger laughed loudly at his own words.

The sensations in Grant's body and mind were those of prey being stalked by a large predator. Fight or flight, his instinct demanded, but neither was an option. Either choice would make matters much worse. He could not win the fight, and running would reward the boys exponentially.

The stalkers sensed the response they were provoking in Grant. They could not resist the clear opportunity to inspire terror in this young stranger.

Meanwhile, Grant's mind rushed to recall what hand gesture he could have made in the malt shop when the boys drove by, or what movement in his walk that might have prompted the particular insult that these self-appointed vigilantes had chosen.

"Keep your hands off her, gay boy!" This time the driver was speaking. This must have been a joke. The insult contradicted itself. Yet, there was a note of seriousness in it. Though his words made no sense, his tone sounded somehow jealous. "Get a life, idiots!" Sophie shouted.

The passenger laughed again, and the muscle car lurched down Main Street with a powerful, hollow-sounding screech from its rear tires.

"You know, I might like living here if it weren't for crap like that happening all the time. I'm sorry about that, Grant."

"Don't worry about it."

"That loser friend of my cousin is always staring at me, but he can't even get out of that car to talk. They're not worth listening to." She paused and then said, thoughtfully, "Are you OK?"

Sophie's question surprisingly angered Grant. He wanted her to assume the boys' accusations to be false and to defend Grant against them. As it was, she did not seem to refute the condemning content of their words, only the spirit in which they had said them. Grant directed his anger, now, at the two boys, "They're the ones who are gay, riding around together in their pretty car!"

Sophie flinched slightly, surprised that Grant chose this particular insult. But she decided not to respond. "We have to turn here," she said.

The abrupt transition between the welcoming malt shop and the threatening trip down the street left Grant emotionally paralyzed. As Sophie said "good-bye" she was visibly sad that a conversation which had transcended time, and the judgment of other people seemed irrelevant now to Grant's frozen gaze. For his part, Grant wanted only to salvage his day, to avoid danger and to complete his experimental solo journey.

Also wanting to preserve something good, Sophie held Grant's wrists and said, as though to wake him, "This is my folk's house, OK? You can come here again if you want to."

Grant felt that he might need to. Already, Larkspur held in tension Grant's deepest longing and also his terror. He would not forget either the total acceptance or the senseless rejection he found here. Sophie saw in Grant someone who may need to move about more than other people, to rely more than most on spontaneous, fringe encounters like theirs today in the malt shop.

It did not take long for Grant to run into Chap on his way back to the mountain. The anger in Chap's frowning mouth was tempered by a glint of understanding in his eyes.

"I ought to skin you alive," he told Grant, with a mix of love and genuine scolding. "How do you propose I tell your parents that I let you escape to a nearby town for a day?"

Grant let Chap's rhetorical question stay in the air between them. He chose to be respect-fully silent for a while.

"I don't expect I'll get off Scott free," Grant admitted.

"No, I don't expect you will. But I am relieved to find you, Grant."

Each walker allowed many footsteps between utterances.

"That was pretty cute the way you cov-ered your tracks up there. I'm good at finding crushed leaves, though. Did you really think you'd shake me?"

"No, I knew I couldn't." Grant waited a moment. "But I did hope I'd slow you down a little."

"About twenty minutes," Chap conceded.

CHAPTER 6

BACK AT CHAP'S HOUSE late that evening, Grant called his parents as his uncle instructed him to do. His mother was shocked and hurt. Grant's parents agreed they would advise Grant of his penance when he returned home.

Grant hung up the phone, grateful for his parents' fairness, and even for their consistency in disciplining him in proportion to his offense.

Chap had brewed the tea already, and the two sat to drink it in the living room.

"Why'd you go?" Chap asked.

Grant thought about this. There was a fifty-fifty mix of interrogation and genuine curiosity in Chap's words and expression. Grant knew he at least owed his uncle an answer.

"I almost couldn't help it," Grant reflected. "I knew it would turn out O.K. even though I felt really bad about running away from you, Chap. It was something I knew I was capable of, so I wanted to try it."

Chap listened.

"It's weird," Grant continued. At church they keep saying that, when we're this age, we're old enough to form our own religious beliefs, to take responsibility for our spiritual lives. So many people treat me like an adult now: my Confirmation teacher, you, my mom and dad, but there's never any room to really live that way. I guess I saw some room here and I took it."

"Makes sense," Chap allowed. "Heck, why do you think I live out here? You'd just better figure out how to find your space without putting all of us through cardiac arrest."

"OK, I will."

The conversation warmed up now, by their words and from the hot tea, so Grant mustered the courage to ask, "Chap, have you ever had a friend who was gay?"

"Yep. Still do." Chap spoke his answers softly. He did not want to offend Grant as he was afraid he had two nights ago.

"Do you mind telling me who?" Grant asked.

"Not at all. I've had several gay friends, one of whom I got to know really well during college."

"So, do you think people choose to be that way, Chap?"

"I used to think that. It was pretty hard for me to understand why anyone would choose that as a lifestyle. But this friend from college, Nate, straightened out my thinking, so to speak." Chap smirked at the irony of his word choice.

"One day we were walking across campus when he said something I'll never forget. This was before I knew that he was gay. I wasn't very tolerant of homosexuals at the time.

"As we were walking, he calmly asked me, 'Chap, do you think that, if you wanted to, you could choose to become gay?' For a minute it freaked me out because I thought he was hitting on me. But I answered him as honestly as I could. I told him, 'No, I know I couldn't choose to be gay.'"

'So what makes you think gay people can choose to be the way they are?'

"I didn't have any answer for that," Chap continued. "I still don't."

"What did you do when he first told you he was gay?" Grant asked.

"We were already close friends, so I assured him this wouldn't change that. Still, I was unsettled. I didn't know what to make of it. I tried to keep an open mind, especially as I started to get to know some of his gay friends. Often when I met them, they seemed unsure of what to make of me. A few looked frightened to be introduced to me when they learned that I wasn't gay. That was a bizarre sensation, to meet someone who automatically feared that I would judge them. It began to sicken me that these guys were scared just to be their true selves around a straight guy. It was then that I realized what pressure gays have to live with. It made me mad. I hated the idea that these kind, good people had to be cautious about simply being themselves in public.

"Anyway, you didn't ask for all that. But that's where I've been and what I've learned. Those friendships have shaped my attitude ever since."

The next morning around ten, Grant's mother and father drove their van onto Chap's gravel driveway. They got out and, with a few subdued laughs and sighs, greeted Chap and briefly discussed Grant's delinquency. Soon they departed. His parents clearly still wanted Grant to feel penitent for his crime. Grant felt prepared to suffer any consequences they might enforce on him. But beneath any guilt over abusing the trust of his loved ones, Grant was deeply grateful for an adventure he would always remember.

CHAPTER 7

IN THE SCHOOL HALLWAYS that next fall, Ryan, a boy in 8th grade like Grant, walked to class with a great, unanswered question. He was a good-looking boy and received attention from girls since his first days at school.

Soon after the year began, he was surprised to find that classmates were not afraid to ask one another terribly personal questions, such as whether they were virgins, if they had entered puberty, or any number of inquiries Ryan may not even understand, much less know how to answer. Up until now, he opted not to say anything in response. On one occasion, he assertively answered, "I don't want to talk about that with you," and walked away. Of course, he heard murmuring behind his back as the two questioners came to their own conclusions.

But there was one question that he wanted to answer for himself. And on this day, as he observed hundreds of other students passing through the campus hallways, he silently asked, "What if I'm gay?" The stakes were clearly high, especially if the answer was, "I am." Among all the personal, even invasive queries his classmates pondered, this one was the most threatening. With a mounting sense of worry, he began to do some research.

He would observe his classmates, both boys and girls, to see what would happen to his feelings. As the passing period was winding down, and the bell would soon call them all back to class, he glanced over toward a set of green lockers that were being opened and slammed shut by the hands of ebullient friends, a mix of boys and girls. He saw one blonde girl whose name, he thought, was Zoe. She turned to her friend, another girl, and shared a joke of some kind so that they both laughed. As he watched the blonde, Ryan felt his soul rest. His gaze stayed with her face. He wanted deeply to belong to her clear, laughing eyes and to her smile. He felt a second desire for her vibrant face to belong to him.

Ryan continued down the hall and suddenly realized that his experiment was concluded. He had never felt that way about any boy, and he had a strong hunch he never would. He softly said to himself, "Thank God. I'm not."

CHAPTER 8

THE NEXT YEARS PASSED SLOWLY for Grant. Society did not allow teenagers to hold meaningful jobs or to exercise judgment on weighty matters. They were not even permitted to vote. The mixed messages made life feel stagnant at times. The preacher would challenge Grant's congregation with invitations to go out and serve, but, being a minor, Grant was not even allowed to serve bowls of soup to strangers at a homeless shelter.

He and his classmates were filled with knowledge and skills, but they would not be encouraged to employ these until after high school, or college, or even graduate school. This left Grant and his classmates to focus almost exclusively on social life. It was the only subject that seemed relevant to them. Decisions concerning relationships carried consequences for today.

And Grant did learn a great deal about social systems. He found that there were mainstream, almost generic characters in the social drama who would be accepted the moment they appeared before their audience. Because he looked carefully and asked questions, he met other people who expressed their personae offstage, or "underground," as they laughingly called it.

But they weren't joking. They were essentially afraid. These friends reminded Grant of Chap's gay college acquaintances who were so wary of being exposed that they were even cautious about meeting Grant's kind uncle.

Other courageous friends were skilled and creative enough to bridge these two worlds. These exceptional ones were interested in broadening the perspective of those in the mainstream, or widening the mainstream itself until it included others who were not at all average, people like Grant.

Grant aspired to be courageous, too. He maintained friendships at church and at school with the easily-accepted and the well-liked, but he also ventured out into social circles that those friends never explored.

When he was 16, he went with several of these friends to a local dance club that was considered to be a fixture in the underground world. Jason, a friend from school, was the one who drove. Jason was one of the bridge people. He also had tremendous energy. It seemed that he avoided being classified by others simply by moving too fast for them.

Jason was refreshingly truthful, but shared ideas in smaller, manageable quantities so that if he offended, it was quick and almost painless. If conversations began to approach personal matters, he would add a witty phrase or two, and then change the subject. It was sometimes difficult for Grant to determine whether Jason was trying to hide from others, or if he simply wanted to keep matters of romance and attraction in perspective.

The others in the car were closer friends to Jason than they were to Grant. So, as they drove to the dance club, Grant remained unsure about why they were going. He also wondered whether Jason had made some kind of assumption about him. But instead of worrying about these questions, Grant decided to assume the best. Jason wanted to have fun, to dance, and that was it. He did not believe life must be categorized before it could be enjoyed.

At the club, the music was pounding. The place looked entirely different from the outside than it did when they walked in. The exterior seemed to be an old, small factory of some sort, with heavy, linear concrete surfaces. Inside, lighting and modern furniture complemented the high-energy music. The building itself seemed to enjoy the celebration hidden within its walls.

Grant was not surprised to see that Jason knew people who were already at the club. Having known Jason now for about two years, Grant anticipated being impressed and surprised by this friend. It was a challenge to keep up with him though, and Grant knew himself well enough to understand that he, much more than Jason, did need certain categories and some grasp of the social terrain in order to comfortably step right in. He noted that the dancers on the floor were nearly all men who clearly enjoyed one another's company.

"I want you to meet some friends!" Jason shouted above the music as he led Grant to a sitting area. To several friends seated on a leather couch Jason shouted, "This is Grant, a friend from school! Grant, this is Darren, Kyle and Jake!" The three young men smiled kindly at Grant. Darren and Kyle were African-American, two of a small number of black patrons at the club that night. Darren seemed to be in his mid-twenties, Kyle, perhaps twenty-one. They both were wearing wrist bands to indicate they had permission to buy alcohol at the club. A half-full glass of beer sat on the coffee table in front of Darren. Jake looked younger, maybe 19, and was white. Grant wondered whether Jason's friends lived somewhere close by the club, someplace downtown.

Soon, Kyle and Jake heard a song they wanted to dance to and slid sidewise off the sofa. Grant sat down in their place. Jason brought Grant a soda. "The first one's on me," he said, and then danced off into the crowd behind him.

The music eventually changed rhythm and was not as loud. Grant and Darren now remained on the sofa watching the dancers. Darren was doubly enigmatic to Grant. Grant had never had a black male friend before. In his biology class, he and a friendly African-American girl enjoyed studying and joking around together, but Grant was unsure how to relate to a black man. In addition, Grant did not know for certain whether or not Darren was gay.

Thankfully, Darren seemed to sense Grant's awkwardness and quietly watched the dancers. His expression even seemed bored at times.

"Do you come here a lot?" Grant asked. He genuinely wanted to know, but quickly felt ashamed of how cliché his question must sound in the context of a dance club.

Darren graciously smiled and said, "My cousin, Kyle, has brought me here a couple of times. You?"

Grant thought Darren must already know the answer. "This is my first time coming here. Jason likes bringing me to places where I don't know what to expect."

Darren smiled and nodded slowly. "As you can see, I don't fit in here very well myself." He paused and looked for Grant's reaction. "You know, because I'm so old." Seeing that Grant didn't dare laugh, Darren's eyes lit up, and he let out a great laugh. Grant ventured a chuckle, feeling reasonably sure that he understood the joke.

"Go ahead and laugh, man! We have to laugh sometimes!" Darren counseled, and continued chuckling. He then leaned back in the sofa, raising one eyebrow at Grant as if to inquire whether he agreed.

Rather than laughing, Grant offered a smile and then became pensive. There was something about Darren's manner that reminded him of someone else. Grant determined that he would solve the puzzle. The familiar gesture had something to do with the eyebrow, Darren's genuine respect and apparent desire to hear Grant's true thoughts.

It was Chap! Chap did the same thing with his eyebrow when he would throw Grant a zinger of a question, the kind that really honored Grant's intelligence and challenged his wits. This is what Grant could focus on now. Rather than acting overly respectful or worried about seeming prejudiced, he would speak with candor to the familiar warmth behind this unfamiliar face.

"I'm from the suburbs," Grant finally offered. "Unfortunately, we don't have much diversity where I come from. I'm a little slow on the uptake with the jokes, I guess."

Darren seemed delighted with Grant's honesty. "Take your time, Grant. It's Grant right?" Grant nodded.

Darren thought for a while and then said, "Grant, I have a theory. Do you want to hear it?"

Grant nodded and continued listening.

"I believe that it takes two steps to get over prejudice. First, you have to believe in your mind that we're all equal, but then you also have to experience a person *as* your equal. Until you do both, you can't really get it."

Grant became aware that the loudness of the club's music forced them to condense their thoughts into focused statements. Each phrase was barely audible, but seemed increasingly meaningful.

"I think I need to take that second step," Grant admitted.

Darren raised his eyebrows and nodded, impressed with Grant's candor, and returned his gaze to the dance floor.

Jason came bouncing over to them at that moment and grabbed Grant's arm. "Come on, you've got to dance at least once while you're here!" Grant stood up to follow Jason, and looked back at Darren to see if he would join them. Darren waved the back of his hand toward the dance floor as if to say, 'Go on, enjoy yourself.'

Grant danced for three songs and then was ready to sit down again. He was aware that men, young and old, were glancing at him. It was gratifying to be noticed and even appreciated by others. At the same time, he was not prepared to convey any message to onlookers that he had not yet confirmed in his own mind.

He went back to the sofa and sat again next to Darren.

"Hey, you're a pretty good dancer for a white guy!" Darren exclaimed, laughing, and warmly slapped Grant's back.

"I'll take that as a compliment. It is a compliment, right?" Grant smirked.

"Of course it is!" Darren answered, playfully acting as though he'd been hurt by Grant's question. Again, Jason, Kyle and Jake stayed on the dance floor, leaving Grant to talk with Darren. After a long while, Darren asked, "So, Grant, what are you doing here?"

Two or three shallower answers passed through Grant's mind. But, instead of offering these, he decided to take advantage of this chance to talk something through. He took a deeper breath before he said his next words: "Jason's been telling me about this place for a while. I have some questions about who I am, and this seemed like a good place to meet other people who might have the same questions. Besides, I like to dance."

"I can see that." Darren was going to let Grant continue if he wanted to.

Over the next few moments, Grant gathered the courage to be even more forthright and finally stated, "Even if I am gay, I don't think it's worth it for me to put that out there as common knowledge. It's easier just to be friends with everyone and not to worry about it."

"And you're able to do that?" Thus far, to Grant's relief, Darren had not flinched. He listened attentively and with respect. He was asking Grant for the truth.

Grant thought back to his friend Marco and the vision he had entertained of a committed relationship with him. He looked around at the dancers and thought how different it felt when other young men admired him. Grant had received such attention from various girls at school and also at church. He always felt, though, that they did not understand. At worst, he thought they were foolish for wasting their attention on him. The men who danced on the floor this evening had at least guessed correctly about Grant's true interests. Though he had only danced three songs, he came back feeling confident and affirmed.

"Yes. I think that for now I can wait."

"You do have that luxury, don't you?" Grant listened to Darren's measured words. "You can wait," Darren continued, "but once you come out, you're going to be a minority, like I am." Darren briefly paused to let his words have full effect. "You can stay "normal" as long as you want." Darren hooked two fingers on each hand to put quotations around the word. "But we don't all have that freedom. Some of us are black."

Darren intentionally spoke those last words with a somewhat haunting smile and with a different accent. It sounded to Grant like the language of a black southern slave he may once have heard speak in a movie.

Darren went on, "The majority of Americans look like you; some look like me. You're bound to seem normal to most people. But as soon as you come out as gay, you're no longer like most people. You become some people. Gays are about ten percent of the population, from what they say. So, welcome to the minority!"

Grant knew Darren was prodding him to think hard about his motivations. He decided to paraphrase Darren's challenging words to make sure that he understood: "You're saying that choosing not to come out is a choice to stay in the majority."

"For you it is, isn't it?"

"I suppose so, but it's not because I think I'm better somehow. It's mostly about self-preservation."

"I can't say that I blame you. If I could preserve myself in the same way, I probably would... No, that's not true." Darren paused as though he was in between phrases in a conversation with himself.

"When I was your age I think I would have. Now I'm proud to be black." Darren then looked forward and spoke more loudly,

"I'm proud to be gay! I'm proud to be black! I'm proud to be all that God's made me to be!" With these words, Darren's proclamation drew some looks and a few smiles from some of the men nearby. Grant felt a little embarrassed. At the same time, he knew that Darren's statement was a sublime conclusion to their dialogue.

Over-hearing Darren's words, Kyle quickly approached and jumped over the coffee table, landing between Grant and Darren. He then kissed his older cousin on the cheek and said, "That's right, Darren, and you should be proud!"

The sunlight that awoke Grant the next morning was a catalyst for his conflicting thoughts to combine and react. The sun-warmed, thick pillow under his head was too luxurious today. Next to the stark urban scenery of last night's adventure, Grant's second story suburban bedroom felt like an overly safe fortress, one he had done nothing to deserve or to build.

His education in school and at church was both a blessing and a curse. Grant was acutely aware that his comfort, even in a middle-class home, was exceptional and, it seemed, unfair. He found himself coveting an understanding of others' experiences, even their suffering. He had thirsted for genuine empathy for the marginalized in his country, and of the impoverished and suffering people around the world. And yet his comfortable, mainstream life seemed to buffer him somehow from any true identification with those who lived life on the margins.

Only Darren's words from last night pierced through Grant's artificially secure world. These words echoed in Grant's mind, "Welcome to the minority." Darren had articulated this last word deliberately, enunciating every syllable. He was aware that Grant would be unprepared to try this descriptor on himself. Last night's conversation represented a bittersweet invitation that Grant had not yet decided to accept. He saw that the path to being misunderstood, isolated, underprivileged, might be as simple as sharing with the world who he honestly was.

Grant smiled at the irony. How fragile this suburban fortress was. The vulnerability of his identity drove him, once again, to ponder ultimate questions. What was on God's mind when he made Grant this way? And wasn't it just like God to silently allow Grant to do the math over time, to discover one Saturday morning that the marginalized "other" whom he had previously pitied was suddenly living beneath his own skin?

Last night Darren had looked beyond Grant's exterior and spoken to him deeply. As he affirmed the person he thought Grant might be, his voice also seemed to caution Grant, "Don't rush it. For you, the trials will come in their own time." Darren, Grant was sure, had battled and been hurt. His deliberately chosen words, his decision not to go out on the dance floor, all of his mannerisms conveyed his desire to treat his own spirit with tenderness, and to be careful with the hearts of others. Grant thanked God for Darren and for this invaluable new wisdom. With it he felt better prepared to navigate human differences while still honoring the truth of his own soul.

CHAPTER 9

GRANT RETURNED SEVERAL TIMES with Jason to the same dance club and to several similar venues downtown. Because he diligently observed his parents' curfews and since they saw no evidence of his turning to drugs or alcohol, Grant's father and mother trusted their son's judgment on those weekend evenings and even lent him a car to drive on occasion.

They also appreciated Grant's faithfulness about attending church on Sunday mornings and the youth group in the evening. Grant valued deeply the friendships he had maintained at church through most of his life. He also knew that the ground rules were different at church than they were at school.

The ridicule and the close scrutiny everyone endured in the high school hallways were generally suspended in the realm of church. The sanctuary, the house of worship itself, was a true place of safety in which pastors and parishioners spoke words of acceptance rather than judgment. Grant was aware that many of his openly gay friends had undergone very different experiences in other churches. Many of those friends were impatient with Grant's own positive attitude about matters of faith. They also reminded him that if he ever came out as a gay person at church, the climate of acceptance might dramatically change. Grant hoped that they were wrong, but he knew better than to assume so.

One Sunday sermon particularly irked Grant. In his message, Reverend Norquist challenged his listeners to invite more and more of themselves to be governed by God's grace and the Spirit's guidance. At one point, Pastor Norquist asked the congregation to examine their own hearts: "Is there some way in which we, as Christians, try to keep some aspect of our lives off-limits to God? How may we include even that part of us in our life of faith?" he asked. He went on to preach about peoples' deep need to become spiritually integrated, to acknowledge that God is already present in every aspect of life, and to learn to celebrate the wholeness of each God-given soul in all its complexity.

Grant felt so stirred up by the message that he slipped into the church office hallways after the service had ended. He found that Pastor Norquist was walking into his office, unfastening a button from his robe as he walked.

To avoid seeming like an intruder, Grant announced his presence saying, "Reverend Norquist, I don't mean to be a pest, but could I ask you something?"

"Sure," Reverend Norquist answered. He was invariably hospitable, but he had also learned to be wary of questioners who approached him immediately after his sermons. Sometimes such queries were more of a confused reaction than a thoughtful response. Still, he answered Grant, "Why don't you sit down while I put my stuff away, OK?"

Grant sat in a chair in the pastor's office. "Your sermon got me thinking a lot today. You know, it's much easier for some people to bring their whole selves before God than for others. There are a lot of people in our church who could never be open with other church members about their whole lives. Some people can't simply invite their whole selves into God's grace. I mean, for some people that might be pretty simple, but for others it's a lot more complicated, isn't it?" Grant could feel his pulse through his flushed face, self-conscious about the demanding tone of his questions, but also still upset by what seemed to him a glaring unfairness in Pastor Norquist's sermon.

"Wow, Grant, you've done it again. That's a good point. Of course, usually I have a little more time before my wife points out the problems with what I've just preached." Though Pastor Norquist was smiling, Grant began to wonder whether his question might be discouraging or even threatening to his pastor.

Pastor Norquist, having hung up his robe and vestments, now dressed in shirt and tie, plopped down in a second chair to offer his full attention to Grant. "I only wish I had a little more blood sugar for this conversation. Give me a minute." He reached up to one of his cabinets, opened the door and pulled out a package of Oreo cookies, placing them on the table between them. "Go ahead." He indicated that Grant could help himself.

On another day, Grant would have made light of Reverend Norquist's choice of office nourishment, but right now he was too determined to hear the answer to his question. He also wasn't one to turn down junk food, so he took two and said, "Thanks."

Reverend Norquist was tired, and he also knew that Grant could hold his own in theological conversation. He felt anxious about whether or not he could adequately answer Grant's dilemma in his present state of mind. He ventured, "You're right, it isn't always safe to be totally open with other church members. I've gotten burned myself, in fact, especially when I've extended challenges to people who aren't ready to hear what I have to say.

"I do believe, though, that God is way better at accepting us than other people are, or than we are at accepting ourselves." Pastor Norquist decided to let this last phrase stand for a moment. He looked for Grant's response but still saw only determination and insistence on understanding.

"As imperfect as the church is," Pastor Norquist continued, "it's a place where we can practice being the way we're intended to be. We give others the opportunity to respond well or badly, and then we try to be patient when they fail us. As unfortunate as it may be when people are judgmental, it's just as bad when we write them off for being that way."

"It's just hard to hear about accepting ourselves," Grant responded, "and being accepted by others when so many people build themselves up by rejecting others. Just think of how many people get their thrills by keeping others out of their 'in' circle," Grant raised his voice somewhat, wanting, suddenly, to preach to this preacher.

"I don't think it's truly thrilling for them, Grant. Most people I've met who judge others harshly seem to have a similar sense of condemnation for themselves. The best we can do, I believe, is to reconcile ourselves with our own minds, to allow God to accept us as we are, and then to start sharing that grace with the rest of the world.

"We do spend a lot of time, as Christians, recounting God's radical acceptance of the unacceptable: Jesus welcomes the outcasts, includes even Judas in his Last Supper, and he prays for the forgiveness of those who put him to death. I believe we have to listen to that message of God's forgiveness and acceptance above the voices of others who reject and condemn us."

Reverend Norquist paused, concerned that he was now answering questions Grant wasn't asking. To remedy his worry, he paused and then asked, "Grant, was there anything else that you wanted to talk about?"

Grant decided to take the pastor's words to mean, "I'd better be going now," though he knew he probably meant, "What else would you like to tell me?" So he answered, "No, Reverend Norquist, that's all for now." With a smile and a tinge of doubt, the pastor, visibly tired, concluded, "My door's always open, OK, Grant?"

"I know. Thank you," Grant replied as he stood up and walked out the door.

CHAPTER 10

IT WAS ANOTHER TWO YEARS until Grant made his next solo visit to Chap's house. It took place during the summer before his senior year in high school and he had already turned 18. Grant had established a strong relationship of trust with his parents, and was allowed to borrow their third, older car to make the hour and a half drive by himself to the rural town in which Chap lived.

Chap was as thrilled as ever to hear the familiar crunch of tires on gravel as Grant pulled-up to the house. Grant was tall and lanky now, and was nearly the mature, poised man that Chap and Grant's parents had always assumed he would become. Chap eagerly awaited whatever philosophical discussion Grant might be capable of now.

But unlike Chap, Grant had not come here primarily to sit and talk. His visit to Chap's house was part of a larger quest. Grant was hoping to use Chap's isolated home and his uncle's accepting nature as a starting point. Chap felt aware that Grant had some complex purpose for his visit, and he was willing to offer his nephew the space to work through the dilemmas of his youth.

As they sat together that evening over tea, Grant looked only occasionally, though lovingly, at Chap's eyes. Chap commented, "They've made some new trails since you were here last. There's a good long one up to Crown Peak if you'd like to try it." The invitation implied Chap's newfound respect for Grant's hiking strength, an adjustment in his perception of Grant since the last visit.

"That's a nice idea, Chap. Thanks. I was wondering, though, would you mind if I take a solo trek?"

"I wondered if you were going to fly the coop again! Now that you're 18, there may not be much I can do to stop you!" Chap observed, and laughed. "Go ahead, Grant. I think you know where I keep my canteens, don't you?"

Now Grant laughed and answered, "I'll get up early like last time. I'll try not to wake you up."

He awoke at five in the morning. Within moments he was energized at the prospect of repeating his actions of five years before. His emotions were rich as he reached into the closet to grab his backpack, just like the last time. He pulled the chain hanging from the closet ceiling to ignite a single light bulb. Scanning the closet to prompt his mind to recall what items to bring, he noticed a flashlight that Chap courteously provided for any guest staying in this room. Grant grabbed it from the shelf where it stood, added it to the backpack and then ventured to the kitchen.

There, on the counter, Grant found a canteen, already full, and trail food laid out, ready for him to pack.

⟨ ⟩

Grant made it out of the house by 5:20, filled with the sense of freedom. He felt grateful to his younger self for braving this same journey half a decade before. The whole mountain ahead of him shrunk slightly under his larger, stronger body. Grant imagined that the earth conspired with him, offering itself to convey him to any destination he might choose. It was this open, accepting, living landscape of brush and forest that his body and mind dearly needed to air his broadest questions.

In under three hours, Grant had summited, and he paused only long enough to eat some jerky, granola, and to drink from the familiar, cold canteen. The mountain top did seem sacred, but Grant had no patience for ritual or reminiscing. With jerky still in his hand, he continued down the trail toward Larkspur.

Now his thoughts raced to construct an updated face for Sophie, who he hoped might miraculously meet him there. After just two hours, he approached Larkspur. He decided not to walk toward Main Street, as the thought of it still recalled deeply imprinted fears. Instead, he went straight to the house Sophie had shown him when she had said he could visit her any time. It was still not quite 11 o'clock.

As he walked, Grant surveyed the neighborhood without turning his head, only scanning with his eyes. Since the last time he visited here, Grant had learned how to function more securely in public. He intentionally offered little information to anyone who would observe him. During school days, Grant had developed a mode of behavior in which he told himself to retract deeper within. If anyone wanted to assault him with words or even blows, they would touch only his shell.

As he walked down the rural neighborhood sidewalk, he went into that protective mental state. He knew, however, that in a town as small as Larkspur, residents could never mistake Grant for some new neighbor whom they had not met, not while he wore a canteen strapped around his shoulder and a pack on his back. Still, Grant walked with the strength of a young man now and was grateful that he would no longer look like a runaway child.

From his vantage point on the sidewalk, he could see part of Main Street directly ahead. He was walking perpendicular to it. He also noticed, parked in front of a small auto parts store, two cars, one of them a large, gray car painted the dull color of primer. Though it was about three blocks away, Grant believed it was the same model as the green muscle car he had seen before.

With the sight of this car, Grant's mind confirmed the instinct of his soul to withdraw to the safety deep within him. This could not, however, prevent his face from tingling with anxiety. The skin under and around his eyes began to swell with blood.

And then the car awoke. Its forceful engine intoned a familiar song of dominating power that repulsed Grant. He watched as the car backed out of its angled space, and then began to move forward. Only it did not proceed smoothly. It slowed very slightly and unexpectedly, as though the driver momentarily changed plans, and then it resumed its speed, heading to Grant's left, farther into downtown Larkspur.

Now Grant's observations were made with his eyes only. He would no longer turn his head. To his left, he saw an open lot, shaded by a large pepper tree. A chain link fence bordered the lot on the far side and separated it from some play equipment which belonged to a small elementary school. Along the base of the fence Grant saw fast food bags and several empty beer bottles. Being several blocks from Main Street, the lot's appearance could understandably be neglected, especially during the summer when the school was not in use. Another block and a half and Grant would reach Sophie's home.

Grant recalled that it was Saturday morning. He had planned his visit with Chap over a weekend so that Chap might not have to take time off from work. Grant felt mildly anxious as he approached Sophie's house that he might find her parents at home now too.

He did not. Instead, an older rendition of the pretty malt shop girl opened the door, disheveled and still dressed in morning pajamas. "It's you! Grant, right? I thought you looked familiar! It is you, isn't it?"

"Yes," Grant laughed. "How are you, Sophie?"

"Well, come in and tell me what's up with you! Are your parents here?"

"No, Dad left early to work at the malt shop, and Mom drove into the city for groceries. She won't be back for a few hours. We can talk here for a while."

Grant and Sophie quickly fell into the spirit of conversation they had begun in the malt shop years before. It was as though they were continuing the same discussion without interruption. Sophie explained that she was home from college and had not yet found a job for the summer.

"So what's your deal, are you running away again?" she asked.

"Kind of. Only I'm 18 now, so technically I can go wherever I want. This time around my uncle knows, but my parents don't, I guess. But they're adjusting pretty well to my independence anyway."

The two spoke for well over an hour before Grant decided to entrust Sophie with more pressing conversation. To approach a deeper topic, Grant began to talk about his friends. He shared about Jason and about Darren, and described the dance clubs. "I can't really understand people who are so out there about being gay," Grant continued. His heart began to race and his mind struggled to make sense of its own thoughts. As though beyond his control, Grant's words no longer sounded true at all. "Sometimes I think those guys are just trying to stir everyone up. I don't know if they really feel that way or if one day they're going to marry and settle down with the girl of their dreams. All I know is that I'm way different from them. Do you know what I mean?"

Sophie became very still, and her brow began to furrow in disbelief at the new direction of their conversation. Then, her face suddenly relaxed and she stood up from the couch she'd been lounging on. "Would you stand up with me for a minute, Grant?"

"OK," Grant looked puzzled, but stood up from the place he'd been sitting on a bar stool near the kitchen.

"Will you just stay there, Grant, and let me try something?"

Grant's heart began to beat faster. Sophie was a beautiful woman, and she was now employing the power of her beauty. Her voice sounded utterly relaxed, in extreme contrast to the anxiety Grant felt throughout his own body. Suddenly, he was terrified that he was about to disappoint her and ruin their friendship.

She approached Grant gradually but steadily until she was able to reach out for both of his hands. She turned her chin up to bring it closer to Grant's, and then she waited, two inches from touching her lips to his.

"Sophie," Grant began.

"Just let me try this," she continued, still relaxed, and she moved her hands up his arms over his elbows.

Grant felt sick.

"No, this won't work! I can't do this with you!" Grant stepped back and turned away from her. He returned to sit on the stool and swiveled the seat away from Sophie's gaze.

Sophie stood in place, unchanged, looking attentively at Grant. For a full minute she was still, silent. As they both remained motionless, Grant readied himself to hear Sophie's anger or embarrassment over the rejection. He felt he deserved to be reprimanded for misleading her somehow, and he was prepared to receive his punishment.

Finally she asked, "That didn't do anything for you, Grant?"

"I'm sorry. No, it didn't, Sophie. You're very beautiful, and I like you very much. But I can't! I don't know why."

"I do," Sophie answered, "You're not made to like me. If you can't, then you can't."

Now Grant returned his gaze to meet Sophie's. If there were any woman he might have passionately kissed, it would have been her. But he knew that to do so would be an awkward, meaningless lie. Clearly, Sophie knew it too. She'd identified the lie before he did. She exposed it for them both. For a moment, they looked silently at each other, long enough for Grant to trust this sensation of being both known and accepted. She gave him all the time he needed and allowed him to break the silence.

"Thank you, Sophie."

"You're welcome."

Grant stood up and walked to his friend and teacher. She opened her arms and held him, and he cried.

CHAPTER 11

GRANT STAYED WITH SOPHIE for another hour and then knew he should start home in order to reach Chap's while it was still light out. Though he had been out of Chap's house much longer than the hike alone would require, he was confident that Chap would not search for him, at least not yet. It was now 3:30 and Grant would just make it to Chap's by nightfall if he started now and traveled steadily.

On the front patio Sophie pulled Grant by the ears so she could kiss his forehead. "Come back in another five years, all right? God knows you'll probably find me in the same place."

"Probably not, but I may come back here anyway." Grant leaned forward and kissed Sophie's cheek. Her love was not the kind that he yearned for, but it had given him the courage to continue his search for it.

He descended the steps from the patio, turned left onto the sidewalk, and headed out of Larkspur, no longer hidden within himself. He began to walk more freely, not as a hiker, or as a newcomer to this town, but as a unique, liberated pilgrim, genuine before himself and the world. His head now turned freely, defiantly from side to side, enjoying his final views of Sophie's street.

Halfway down the second block from her house, Grant's spirits plummeted as he identified the rumbling engine sounds, and then saw a chrome front bumper emerge from behind the corner house to the left of the next intersection. It moved very slowly, and before Grant could see anyone in the front seats, he started across the street to avoid walking directly toward the car.

As he traversed the pavement, the car rolled slowly, straight through the stop sign and into the intersection, the side of the car now blocking the street. Grant could now see, with his peripheral vision, two figures seated in the front. They were familiar, though bigger now than he remembered them.

Feeling his face pulsing as intensely as the idling engine, Grant walked in a straight line. He would not turn or run until he knew he could make it to the trailhead before his enemies, and to do this he would have to get past them. Grant would not give them the pleasure of chasing him back through town with their giant steel machine.

Now, he walked directly in front of the car, gambling on their reluctance to run him over. In another ten yards he would have run for the trailhead, but suddenly, the car halted, parked with impunity in the middle of the intersection, and the driver and passenger quickly emerged from either side.

"What were you doing in Sophie's house? Are you trying to give her AIDS?"

Like sheepdogs, the two men flanked Grant and blocked his path to the trail. As the two walked toward him, Grant was forced to turn the corner, heading perpendicular now to Sophie's street and farther from her house. Soon he would be near the back fence of the school he had seen before, and the large pepper tree. Then he stopped, experimenting with his assailants to see whether they would only talk and allow him to pass between them toward the trail. Reflexively, the men stepped toward each other and closed the space between them. They progressed toward Grant, pushing him back like a bulldozer.

"Let me go," Grant attempted.

"We haven't touched, you, homo," said the one who Grant recalled to be Sophie's cousin.

"Let me get by you."

"First, we want to talk to you," said the cousin's friend.

"Then talk to me right here." Again Grant stopped walking.

But the two answered with their bodies, each grabbing an arm and pushing Grant toward the fence below the pepper tree. Grant struggled to pull his arms free, but the two had fiercely gripped his upper arms.

"You need to stay away from Sophie, understand?" With this order, the cousin's friend threw Grant backward with the full force of his jealousy and spite, so that Grant stumbled, tripped and sat down hard in the dirt with his back against the chain-linked fence.

"Fine, I'm trying to go home now!" Grant started to his feet but was shocked by a fist's concussion on the left side of his face, knocking him abruptly back to the ground.

At this moment he heard the piercing, wavering voice of a woman running toward them, "What the hell are you doing to him?" The three men jerked their heads toward the street corner where Sophie had picked up a large stick and was running in her pajamas to confront Grant's assailants. Grant took the opportunity to scramble back to his feet, lunge between the two men and turn to face them again. Now standing, he could choose whether to stay and help Sophie confront his assailants, or to run, unobstructed, toward the trailhead. The cousin and friend stepped toward Grant as though to recapture him, but Sophie had arrived, brandishing her stick, and stood between them and Grant.

"Get out of here, Grant, now!" she yelled with her back to him. She held the stick with both hands as she stared the two men down. Then, again she commanded Grant, "Go!"

But Grant could not leave. Now Sophie's cousin spoke, patronizingly, saying, "Sophie, just relax." He stepped forward as though to grab the stick. Sophie swung it, striking her cousin's wrist so that he was forced to jump back.

At the same moment a siren blared, full volume, as a patrol car roared around the corner toward the four of them.

"Now, go, Grant! Please!" Grant wanted badly to run, to return to the safety of Chap's home, but he knew he must defend Sophie's actions to the police, just as she had defended him. The officer swiftly stopped his brilliantly lit car and, holding a club, demanded that Sophie put down the stick that she still gripped tightly.

Grant stepped forward and said, "They were attacking me, officer. Sophie was only trying to help." The next moment, a second patrol car sped in from the opposite direction and blocked the other end of the street. "All of you, sit down on the ground," the first officer ordered. "You're going to tell me everything that happened."

It was another half hour before Grant was permitted to go home. The two officers decided to take Sophie and the two men in for further questioning and to determine how to avoid additional conflicts between them.

"I'm so sorry, Grant," Sophie said as she went to get in the patrol car.

"Thank you, Sophie, for everything." He was no longer afraid to be seen, and he smiled at her with courageous love. His greatest fears, or at least some of them, were already realized this afternoon, and, thanks to Sophie, he had survived and was free to begin his hike home.

As Sophie was still standing next to the car, he approached her to hug her once again. He did so, fully aware that the warped jealousy of her cousin must have been aroused, but this would no longer determine Grant's behavior. He squeezed Sophie strongly and said, "I won't waste what you've given me today."

With an appreciative, but pensive smile, Sophie finally ducked into the patrol car and faced forward. Grant was aware, by his peripheral vision, that his two assailants were being seated in the other car. He did not indulge them with eye contact. Grant also wanted his last impression to be of Sophie's face, and her mild expression of pride, as she rode in her pajamas to the sheriff's station.

CHAPTER 12

THE STILLNESS OF LATE AFTERNOON provided Grant a perfect quiet in which to walk and think. It would not be long until dusk, the sacred hour when days find their meaning. The sting below Grant's left eye, and the stiffness settling into his jaw periodically caused feelings of terror to resurface with residual impulses of self-preservation. But as his path changed from pavement, to gravel, to dirt, Grant felt a new a sense of euphoria. The threat of darkness or wild animals was miniscule in comparison with the confused destructive nature of some humans.

The walk gave room for Grant's imagination to wander and to replay the assault he had suffered. He repeated the scene in his mind, picturing how he might have responded if he had been armed with a knife or even a gun. As these darker thoughts came and went, he concluded that he had responded as well as he could have to his attackers. Their destructive nature had been exposed, vented and arrested. Now he left town just as he had entered Larkspur, only with a new burn pulsing in his left cheek.

As Grant approached the peak of the mountain, he realized he would be rewarded with more sunlight at the summit. He would no longer being shielded from the sun by the mountain itself. When he arrived there, he found the sun preparing to set, clear on the horizon on this dry summer night. The breezes had all been stilled and the mountain top, adorned with granite boulders and hearty shrubs, seemed like an inviting parlor, tastefully arranged to receive its guest.

One of the larger boulders offered an ideal seat from which Grant could observe the sunset. He thought momentarily about checking the flashlight batteries, but decided, instead, to trust Chap's track record of keeping equipment always ready to use. Grant pulled the canteen from his shoulder and finished all but a few swallows of water. He had a sense that he had been trusting Chap's silent assistance all day long.

Then he thought of Larkspur. There was no particular reason why he should not have been killed there today. There was also no reason why he should have been so warmly received and loved by a near stranger. Tears of gratitude welled in Grant's eyes as he sensed the cosmos itself had led him and had protected him. He offered prayers of thanks that the battles waged for so long within his mind had now been acted out externally. His dilemmas were dignified somehow by the fact that actual enemies and friends played the roles he had scripted in his head hundreds of times in the past.

Today he had been given a place to spill his inner tensions outward, and he remained himself, a child of God. He felt affirmed in his instincts and in the way he had reacted to danger. Perhaps, back on the west side of these mountains he could now persevere, even if he were known, accepted or threatened again.

The granite boulder which had been warmed by the sun when Grant first sat on it now began to cool. It remained warmer than the evening air, though, and Grant felt nostalgic about leaving it. The mountain itself seemed to be his friend now, the most sacred place he knew. Though the sun had set, he did not feel anxious about descending the trail in the dark. The trail was almost memorized now and he would put off using artificial light as long as possible. He knew that food and welcome awaited him at the warm cabin below.

CHAPTER 13

SEATED ON THE FRONT PORCH under a dim lantern, Chap did not notice, at first, that Grant's left cheek was swollen and bruised. Only when they walked inside did he say, "Dear God, boy, let me get you some ice! Where did you go today? Come in here and sit down."

Once his nephew was resting with a bag of ice on his face, he brewed Grant some tea. When it was finished, he also brought a couple of pills to assuage the pain of the wound and the headache that accompanied it.

"So, Larkspur again?" he asked.

"Yeah. I wanted to see an old friend."

"Maybe you could tell me what happened to your eye so that I don't look too foolish when your parents ask."

"All right."

Grant described his journey, but not in great detail. To explain the beating he'd received, he emphasized the boys' jealousy and protective-ness of Sophie and didn't mention any specific epithets that they had shouted at him. He did include, though, Sophie's courageous actions, and the fortunate conclusion due to the sher-iff's arrival.

Chap's expression remained encouraging and affirming, but he was on the verge of tears. There was another side to this story which nei-ther of them would tell that evening. It was the age-old tragedy of the powerful pushing down the one who is different, merely because they can, and because they are weak within.

For this reason, the tears which Chap would not let escape in Grant's presence, but only later, were also mixed with gratitude. The more beautiful spirit of his nephew had overcome his enemies. By the providential love of a new friend and the strong foundation of Grant's family, he was equipped, now, to continue his travels.

"Thanks for the canteen, Chap, and the trail food."

"You bet, Grant. I'll go heat up a bowl of stew for you."

After his late dinner of stew and bread, Grant felt fatigue settle upon him heavily. He headed directly for the guest room and, without undressing, lay down on the bed. But though his body was exhausted, his mind would not yet rest. He thought again and again of Sophie's face. In his mind's eye, her expression demanded something of him, as it had when she tested him in her house earlier that day.

He sat up in bed, and felt his mild headache increase slightly. Now Grant was looking directly at the closet door which stood ajar. Suddenly, he saw the irony of what he was looking at and laughed, slightly, as though at some unspoken joke. Then his face grew serious and resolute. He stood up from the bed, feeling his headache increase again, and placed his hand on the closet door's inner door knob.

Grant backed slowly inside and, leaving the light off, he pulled the door shut and sat down on the cool wooden floor. His journey today was overwhelmingly meaningful, but it was not yet complete. In the blackness of the closet, Sophie's face appeared more clearly than ever. He began to want for himself what Sophie wanted for him. Grant also heard, again and again, the cry of her voice, and saw that fearless, running young woman, ready to battle the forces that had pushed Grant down. Legs crossed, he buried his face in his hands, filled with gratitude.

But gratitude was not enough. Sophie's gift of love, her sacrifice, not only defended him from harm, but liberated him. Suddenly, Grant sat up and smiled. He perceived in the black air before his eyes that he was free to walk out through this door as the man he truly was – a gay man, a Christian man, a unique child of God.

Now he felt he could receive every sacrifice of love he had been given. He thanked God for Sophie's inexplicable actions. He remembered the nurture of his parents and Uncle Chap. And he reflected on the ancient mystery of the Redeemer who died speaking words of forgiveness, and whose face, like Sophie's, beckoned Grant to be whole and to truly live.

Grant's tired, bruised body was filled with love. He raised himself with a new strength to his feet and smiled, whimsically at the closet door. He placed his hand on the doorknob, and he walked out.

THE END

AFTERWORD:
A CALL TO COMPASSION

THROUGH RECENT DEBATES, church splits and dramatic changes in our laws, through all the painful discussions society has endured, something good has happened: we have awakened to the need to show compassion to our neighbors, including those who are gay, lesbian, bisexual and transgender.

Thankfully, it has become less and less acceptable to refer to LGBT neighbors with harmful epithets and insults. Increasingly, our eyes are being opened to the genuine humanity in neighbors who are different from ourselves.

During an intense debate on these subjects at the seminary I attended, a wise and humble conservative Christian friend asked Sue, an openly lesbian student, what counsel she might offer if a gay or lesbian church member approached her for pastoral support.

Sue's answer was, "First make sure that your church member knows he or she is not a monster." Sue went on to explain that once individuals realize they are gay, they begin wrestling with all the voices, internally and externally condemning them as abnormal and freakish. It is especially difficult for such persons, she said, to stabilize their thinking and hold fast to their identity as beloved children of God. First and foremost, she said, pastors should assure their parishioners that they are beloved children of God.

Whether or not Christians believe homosexuality is a sin, we can at least do this much. We can show compassion and begin to reverse the historic treatment of homosexual and transgender neighbors as freaks or deviants who willfully rebel against God's will.

Consistently, Jesus addressed people as individuals and refused to treat them simply as members of one category or another. Above all, we must show God's compassion. Thankfully, such grace is being shown more and more in our world, even among those who starkly disagree.

APPENDIX:
TO GRANT, FROM PASTOR NORQUIST

DEAR GRANT,

Recently I've been thinking back to the rich conversations you and I have had in my office. I want to thank you for your courage and wisdom in sharing your deepest concerns with me. It's only through such honest and vulnerable searching that any of us grows in faith and wisdom.

During those talks, you asked such good questions about the Bible and homosexuality, I'd like to further explain why I believe it is biblically sound to accept homosexual people as equals.

At times we hear people say things like, "The Bible is against it (homosexuality)." Such statements show that the speaker has probably not read the Bible carefully enough. The truth is, there is no New Testament command concerning homosexual behavior. There are a few New Testament references to the topic, like Romans 1:26-27, where the apostle Paul decries the way "women exchanged natural intercourse for unnatural, and in the same way also the men, giving up natural intercourse with women, were consumed with passion for one another." But while these verses portray homosexual behavior in a negative light, still, neither St. Paul nor any other New Testament writer articulates any commandment against homosexual behavior.

The one place that the Bible directly prohibits homosexual behavior is in the Old Testament, in the book of Leviticus (Lev. 18:22). As you and I discussed, this commandment addresses only a behavior. It does not address the issue of inherent sexual orientation which we have learned so much about in recent years.

What's more, we must remember that, from a Christian perspective, Levitical law is not binding.

We learn this in the Book of Acts in the 15th chapter when Peter, Paul and James issue a ruling for the early church that new converts to the Christian faith should not be required to abide by the whole law of Moses. They proclaim that neither Gentile nor Jewish converts to Christian faith should be required to abide by all the laws of the Old Testament, also known as the Hebrew Scriptures. Instead, Peter declares, "We will be saved through the grace of the Lord Jesus" (Acts 15:11).

St. Paul teaches a similar lesson in his letter to the Romans when he explains that Christians live "not under law but under grace" (Rom. 6:14). In his letter to the Galatians Paul further explains that those who follow Jesus now live under the law of faith rather than the law of the Old Testament. This new law, Paul explains, allows followers of Jesus to welcome all people, whether Jew or Greek, slave or free, male or female (Gal. 3:23-29).

So, Grant, the fact is that our Christian scriptures offer no clear commandment for us regarding the subject of homosexuality. At the same time, we do see that the Gospel inspired the first Christians to accept more and more diverse neighbors in Jesus' name.

It's important, though, that when we discover a topic like this one which is not clearly addressed in our scriptures, we do not then close our Bibles. We should keep reading for the greater principles which should guide our actions and ethics concerning LGBT persons. We must look to the way that Jesus lived and loved the people of his time. And we must look up to the highest principles of scripture, such as Jesus' command: "Do to others as you would have them do to you; for this is the law and the prophets" (Matt. 7:12). The whole essence of God's law, and all of the scriptures, is accomplished when we follow this Golden Rule.

So, just as we hope people would learn to accept us as we are, we should accept others as they are. Jesus' Golden Rule teaches that we should treat every neighbor, in both our behavior and in our public policies, just as we wish to be treated. If we want the freedom to fall in love with, and to commit ourselves permanently to another person, we should not prevent others from enjoying the same kind of love and commitment.

Once again, thank you for asking the questions which so many people are seeking answers to, including myself. Together, we stand a much greater chance of discerning God's will for us all.

Please keep in touch. I hope that our conversation continues!

Your Friend in God's Love,

Mike Norquist

ABOUT THE AUTHOR

JAMES DOLLINS IS a United Methodist pastor who feels strongly that all people should know the acceptance and love of God. A graduate of UC Berkeley and Garret-Evangelical Theological Seminary, Rev. Dollins has been blessed with pivotal friendships with gay and lesbian Christians who courageously accept themselves, and who proclaim that God loves them just as they are.

Spending much of his career in the area of youth ministry, Rev. Dollins has witnessed the urgency of self-acceptance for youth and young adults, and the dangerous stress that self-rejection causes. He hopes that his writing will encourage more young people to receive God's grace.

Rev. Dollins, with his wife and two sons, lives in Anaheim, California where he serves as the pastor of Anaheim United Methodist Church.

James D. Dollins
jamesddollins@gmail.com

Made in the USA
Las Vegas, NV
25 July 2023

75212389R00066